Franklin's Birthday Party

From an episode of the animated TV series *Franklin*
produced by Nelvana Limited, Neurones France s.a.r.l.
and Neurones Luxembourg S.A.

Based on the Franklin books by
Paulette Bourgeois and Brenda Clark.

TV tie-in adaptation written by Sharon Jennings and
illustrated by Sean Jeffrey, Mark Koren and Jelena Sisic.

Based on the TV episode *Franklin's Birthday Party*, written by
Frank Diteljan.

Franklin is a trademark of Kids Can Press Ltd.
The character of Franklin was created by Paulette Bourgeois and Brenda Clark.
Text © 2001 Context*x* Inc.
Illustrations © 2001 Brenda Clark Illustrator Inc.

Kids Can Press acknowledges the financial support of the Ontario Arts Council,
the Canada Council for the Arts and the Government of Canada, through
the BPIDP, for our publishing activity.

Kids Can Press Ltd.
29 Birch Avenue
Toronto, ON M4V 1E2

www.kidscanpress.com

Edited by Tara Walker

Printed in Hong Kong by Wing King Tong Company Limited

CM 01 0 9 8 7 6 5 4 3 2 1
CDN PA 01 0 9 8 7 6 5 4 3 2 1

Canadian Cataloguing in Publication Data

Jennings, Sharon
    Franklin's birthday party

(A Franklin TV storybook)
Based on characters created by Paulette Bourgeois and Brenda Clark.

ISBN 1-55074-882-3 (bound)   ISBN 1-55074-880-7 (pbk.)

I. Jeffrey, Sean. II. Koren, Mark. III. Sisic, Jelena. IV. Bourgeois, Paulette.
V. Clark, Brenda. VI. Title. VII. Series: Franklin TV storybook.

PS8569.E563F733 2001   jC813'.54   C00-932878-5
PZ7J429877Fr 2001

Kids Can Press is a Nelvana company

Franklin's Birthday Party

Based on characters created by
Paulette Bourgeois and Brenda Clark

Kids Can Press

FRANKLIN could count by twos and tie his shoes. He knew the days of the week and the months of the year. Soon it would be his birthday. Franklin was counting the days to the best birthday party ever.

Franklin looked at the photos in the family album.

"Last year I had a treasure hunt for my birthday," he said. "And the year before that I had a costume party."

"What do you want to do this year?" asked his mother.

"I'm not sure," replied Franklin. "But it's going to be the best party ever."

The next day, Franklin invited all of his friends to his birthday.

"What are we doing at your party?" asked Bear.

"I don't know yet," answered Franklin. "But I want to do something really fun!"

Franklin's friends had lots of ideas.
"How about minigolf?" said Snail.
"Or bowling?" suggested Fox.
"Waterslides are fun," said Goose.
"I like squirt tag," said Badger.

Franklin said these were all great ideas.

"But you'll have to choose, Franklin," insisted Beaver. "We can't do everything."

Franklin thought for a moment.

"We can if we go to Tamarack Play Park," he replied. "They have *everything* there!"

Everyone was excited.

Franklin ran home and told his parents the good news.

"Tamarack Play Park will be lots of fun," agreed his father.

"And I've already invited everyone!" Franklin announced.

"Oh dear," said his mother.

Franklin's parents explained the problem.

"Tamarack Play Park is expensive, Franklin," said his father. "We can only take two of your friends."

Franklin felt terrible.

His mother gave him a hug. "I'm sure your other friends will understand."

Franklin wasn't so sure.

Franklin didn't play with his friends for the rest of the day. He stayed in his room and thought about his party. He really wanted to go to Tamarack Play Park. But how could he pick just two of his friends? What would he tell the others?

Franklin sighed. This was *not* going to be the best birthday ever.

At supper that night, Franklin told his parents that he wanted everyone at his party.

"You can have all your friends if your party's in the backyard," his mother suggested.

"But there's so much to do at Tamarack Play Park," said Franklin.

"Too bad we can't bring Tamarack to the backyard!" laughed his father.

Hmm, thought Franklin.

"Maybe we can!" he exclaimed.

Franklin and his parents were busy all that
week. They spent lots of time in the toolshed and
in the basement and outside in the yard. They
made trips to the hardware store and to the
party shop.

Franklin didn't tell anyone what they were
doing.

By noon on Saturday, all of Franklin's friends had arrived for the party.

"When are we going to Tamarack?" asked Bear.

"Well ... we're not," answered Franklin.

"What do you mean?" demanded Beaver.

Franklin took a deep breath and explained.

"I wanted *all* of you at my party," he finished. "So ... follow me!"

Franklin led the way to the backyard.
"Welcome to Turtle Play Park," he announced.
"Wow!" said everyone.

All afternoon, Franklin and his friends played minigolf and lawn bowling.

They ran through the sprinkler and slid down the slide into the pond.

They played squirt
tag and pin the tail on
the turtle. There was
lots of food and games
and prizes.

Soon it was time for cake and ice cream.
Everyone gathered around Franklin and sang
"Happy Birthday" with loud and cheerful
voices. Afterwards, Franklin opened his gifts,
and each one was just right.

When all of his friends had gone home, Franklin thanked his parents.

"Was it the best birthday party ever?" they asked him.

"It sure was," said Franklin.

Then he grinned. "Until next year!"